Advance Praise for
What Do You Say to a Dragon?

Our best stories are the ones where we aren't afraid any longer. This book will help us understand what we have been telling ourselves and decide whether it's really true.

BOB GOFF, author of the *NYT* bestsellers *Love Does*; *Everybody, Always*; and *Dream Big*

In addition to being a fun rhyme and an easy-to-read story, I love how Lexi teaches courage—not through bravado or fear denial, but through intentionally cultivating curiosity, empathy, and self-awareness. There is so much wisdom within these pages, not just for our littles, but for us bigs, too.

LIZ FORKIN BOHANNON, CEO of Sseko Designs and author of *Beginner's Pluck*

I received my copy of *What Do You Say to a Dragon?* during my nine months of being quarantined here on my farm in Tennessee. I believe that everything happens for a reason. The timing of reading this story is right on! With all that is taking place in my personal and professional life, as well as what is happening to friends and family and to the rest of the world, we are all navigating uncharted waters.

I love this book so much! The story applies to every part of my life. Thank you for the reminder that when I face what is scary and still feel afraid, I can build up the courage to stand and be brave! And yes, the next time a dragon shows up in my life, I will say, "Welcome, my friend, I've got questions for you!" Amen.

WYNONNA JUDD, award-winning singer-songwriter

A powerful and helpful gift for the children in my life about a truth I am still learning myself.

WM. PAUL YOUNG, author of *The Shack*

If nighttime fears are dragons, maybe this charming book is not only for children who are afraid of the dark but also for the parents and grandparents who read it to them. What an effective way to reinforce a holy promise: "You shall not be afraid of the terror [dragon] by night, nor of the arrow that flies by day" (Psalm 91:5, NKJV).

GLORIA GAITHER, award-winning singer-songwriter

Oh, I love this book. What a wonderful world it would be if we could befriend those who scare us.

MARK LOWRY, singer-songwriter

Lexi Young Peck gives both parents and children the tools to effectively move beyond obstacles and fears that seem like monsters. We were able to see the principles found in *What Do You Say to a Dragon?* in action when we read the book with our grandchildren. They were able to clearly understand the book and explain it.

DENISE AND KEVIN JONAS SR.

My daughter and I love *What Do You Say to a Dragon?* The simple lesson of pushing past our fear and prejudice to find out what's underneath isn't just for kids. If grown-ups applied this to our daily interactions, we'd find ourselves in a much happier world.

BETHANY JOY LENZ, TV and stage actor, singer

WITHDRAWN
CHARLESTON COUNTY LIBRARY

What do you say to a Dragon?

**A Story about Facing
Fear and Anxiety**

by Lexi Young Peck

illustrations by Wendy Leach

TYNDALE
KIDS

Tyndale House Publishers
Carol Stream, Illinois

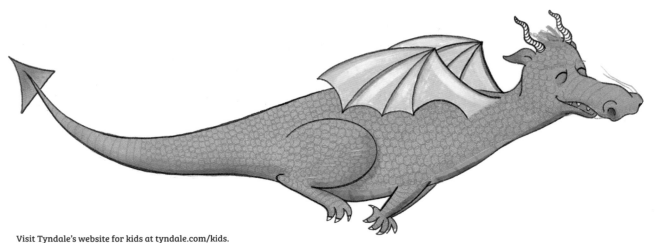

Visit Tyndale's website for kids at tyndale.com/kids.

Visit the author online at lexipeck.com.

TYNDALE is a registered trademark of Tyndale House Ministries. The Tyndale Kids logo is a trademark of Tyndale House Ministries.

What Do You Say to a Dragon?: A Story about Facing Fear and Anxiety

Copyright © 2021 by Alexandra Peck. All rights reserved.

Illustrations by Wendy Leach/Astound. Copyright © Tyndale House Publishers. All rights reserved.

Designed by Jacqueline L. Nuñez

Edited by Crystal Bowman and Sarah Rubio

The author is represented by Ambassador Literary Agency, Nashville, TN.

For manufacturing information regarding this product, please call 1-855-277-9400.

For information about special discounts for bulk purchases, please contact Tyndale House Publishers at csresponse@tyndale.com, or call 1-855-277-9400.

Library of Congress Cataloging-in-Publication Data
Names: Peck, Lexi Young, author.
Title: What do you say to a dragon? : a story about facing fear and anxiety
  / Lexi Young Peck.
Description: Carol Stream, Illinois : Tyndale House Publishers, [2021] |
  Summary: A child gains courage after facing a scary dragon in a dream.
Identifiers: LCCN 2020021213 | ISBN 9781496451040 (hardcover) | ISBN
  9781496451057 (board)
Subjects: CYAC: Stories in rhyme. | Fear--Fiction. | Courage--Fiction. |
  Dragons--Fiction.
Classification: LCC PZ8.3.P2757 Wh 2021 | DDC [E]--dc23
LC record available at https://lccn.loc.gov/2020021213

Printed in China

27	26	25	24	23	22	21
7	6	5	4	3	2	1

For Vivian and Xander, the ones who showed me how brave I could be. I love you.
—Mom

One night I woke up from a terrible dream.
I sat straight up in bed as I started to scream.
"Help, Daddy! Help, Mommy! I'm scared! Please come quick!

I had a bad nightmare,
and now I feel sick."

In came my dad, with my mom close behind.
It was late, they were tired, but they didn't mind.
They sat on my bed and asked, "Honey, what's wrong?"

"I saw a big dragon!
He was scary and strong!"

I pulled up my blankets tight over my head.
My mom moved them gently and then softly said,
"Tell us about him—what terrified you?"

4

I almost screamed, **"NO!"** But I knew what to do.

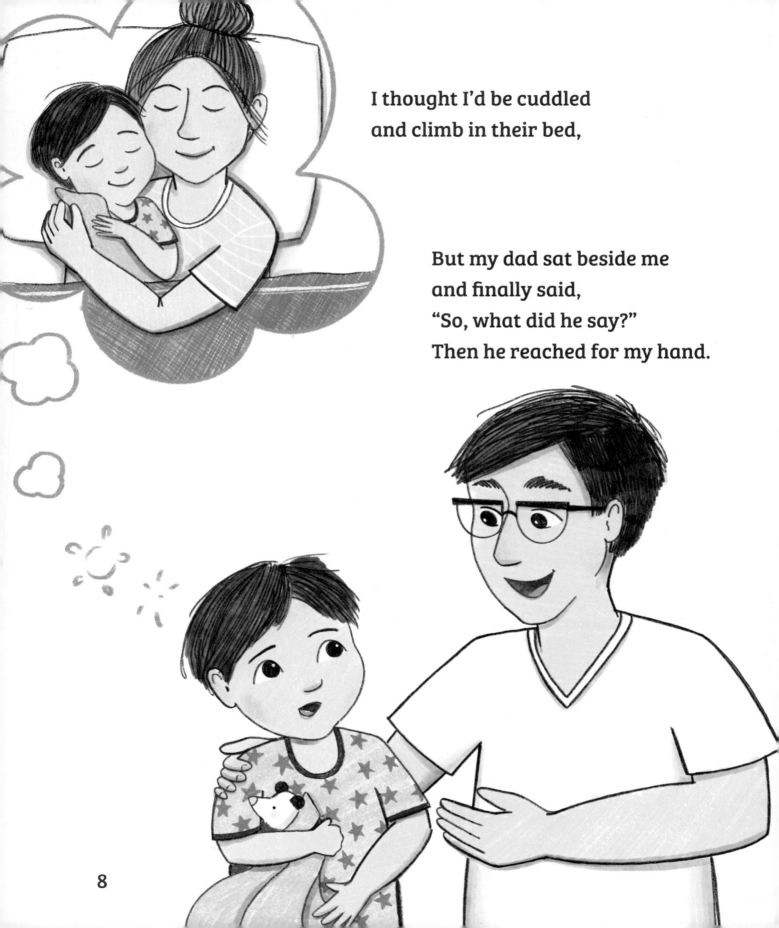

I thought I'd be cuddled
and climb in their bed,

But my dad sat beside me
and finally said,
"So, what did he say?"
Then he reached for my hand.

8

"The dragon?" I wondered.
"I don't understand."

"Yes, did you ask him why he was there?"

"Ask the dragon a question?
Oh no, I don't dare."

11

"You taught me never to go after dangerous things.
You want me to walk toward them inside of my dreams?"
"You're so clever." Dad smiled. "What you're saying is true.
When you are in danger, that is what you should do.
From all unsafe things run to Mom or to Dad."

"But in dreams, it is different.
You can face what is bad."

13

"So, here is the thing that I want you to try:
be strong and be bold—look him right in the eye.
Talk to that dragon, and maybe you'll see
he isn't as scary as he seems to be."

"Close your eyes and let's practice—let's do it tonight."
I was willing to try, so I closed my eyes tight.
"Now, imagine the dragon you saw in your dream—
is he big, is he scary, is he wild or mean?"

15

"He is big and scary," I said to my dad.
"But his eyes are all red, and his face is so sad."
"Then talk to the dragon. Be brave and be strong."
So I said,

"Hey there, Dragon,
please tell me what's
wrong."

The dragon was quiet, then to my surprise
he started to speak with big tears in his eyes.
"Today was a day that was horribly bad.
I roar and breathe fire whenever I'm sad.
I'm not a bad dragon; I just had a bad day . . .
I don't want to scare others when I feel this way."

21

I told Mom and Dad what that big dragon said.
They gave me a hug and a kiss on my head.
"Good job, little one! We are so proud of you!
Facing fear is not easy, but it's important to do."

22

They went back to their room, and I fell back asleep.
The dragon and I became great friends that week.

That monster, my dragon,
taught me something brand new.
I am strong, bold, courageous, and curious, too.

24

He's not the only one
who has power, no way!

I can do what is hard at
the end of the day!

When we face what is scary,
we may still feel afraid,
but it builds up our courage to
stand and be brave.
So next time a dragon shows
up in your room, say,

"Welcome, my friend,
I've got questions
for you."

26

Other Heart-Changing Books from Tyndale Kids

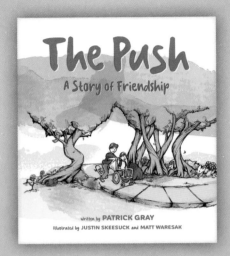

We all have something to offer each other, and we are better together. Based on Patrick Gray and Justin Skeesuck's real-life friendship.

A testament to the power one person has to change the world and influence others.

Your Chooser says, "Yes!"
Your Chooser says, "No."
Your Chooser says, "There's someplace I'd like to go."

A tenderhearted anthem teaching little girls that they have immeasurable worth.

AVAILABLE AT YOUR FAVORITE BOOKSELLER

CP